Andi's
Scary School Days

Circle C Beginnings Series

Circle C Beginnings

Andi's Scary School Days

Susan K. Marlow
Illustrated by Leslie Gammelgaard

Kregel
Publications

Andi's Scary School Days
©2011 by Susan K. Marlow

Illustrations ©2011 by Leslie Gammelgaard

Published by Kregel Publications, a division of Kregel, Inc., P.O. Box 2607, Grand Rapids, MI 49501.

ISBN 978-0-8254-4183-7

Printed in the United States of America
11 12 13 14 15 / 5 4 3 2 1

Contents

New Words

blackboard   a large, smooth, dark surface to write on with chalk

livery stable   a place in town where people can rent horses and buggies

ma'am   like "Mrs."; a polite way to talk to a lady

pinafore   a ruffled apron worn over a dress

pupil   a student in school

scaredy-cat   someone who is afraid

slate   a small blackboard each pupil uses to write their lessons with chalk

straw   the dried, pale-yellow stems left over from wheat or oats

tardy   late

tomboy   a girl who likes to dress and play like a boy

Chapter 1

Hide and Seek

Andi Carter peeked over the half-door of her horse's stall.

"Nobody's coming," she whispered. "This is a good hiding place. Maybe I'm safe."

Andi's baby horse, Taffy, swished her tail. She nibbled Andi's hair. Then she stamped her hoof and whinnied.

Let's go play! Taffy seemed to be saying.

"Shhh!" Andi said. "You have to be quiet, so nobody finds me."

Taffy's mama, Snowflake, turned her large, white head and looked at Andi.

"You have to be quiet too," Andi said. "I can't come out until the buggy drives away."

Just then Andi heard the barn door creak open. She heard footsteps coming closer.

Uh-oh!

Andi ducked into a corner. She wiggled down in the golden straw and squeezed her eyes shut. She tried not to breathe . . . or sneeze.

"Hey, Andi!"

The loud voice made Andi jump. Her eyes popped open.

Her friend Riley was poking his head over the stall door.

"What are you doing in here?" he asked. "Your brother is looking all over for you."

Andi frowned. Nosy ol' Riley!

Maybe this is not a good hiding place, after all, she thought.

"Shhh!" Andi told Riley in a loud whisper. "I'm hiding. I can't let Justin find me."

"Too late," Andi's big brother Justin said. He came up behind Riley and opened the stall door. "I found you. It's time to go." He smiled.

Andi didn't move. Her stomach felt fluttery. Like a hundred butterflies were flying around in there.

It was not a good feeling.

"You and Melinda can go," Andi said. "I'm staying home with Riley and Taffy."

"Oh, no, you're not," Justin said.

He walked right over to Andi's hiding place and picked her up.

"Put me down!" Andi hollered. She squirmed to get free.

But her big brother was too strong.

"Today is your first day of school," Justin said. "You don't want to be late."

He walked out of the barn and into the bright sunshine.

"I *can't* go to school," Andi said. "I have to train Taffy. I have to take care of Coco. I have to—"

"All little girls and boys must go to school," Justin said. He kept walking.

"Riley doesn't have to go to school," Andi said.

She twisted around and saw Riley running to the cookhouse. "He gets to help his Uncle Sid with ranch work."

"Only until Riley goes home," Justin said. "Then he'll have to go back to school."

Justin was right about that. Riley was just staying on the ranch until his mother got well.

Justin carried Andi to the buggy. He set her down next to Melinda, Andi's big sister.

Eleven-year-old Melinda looked fresh and pretty—like always. A big, blue bow tied back her hair. She held her school books in her lap. She was smiling.

But Melinda's smile didn't last long.

She saw Andi and gasped. "What happened to *you*? You're all rumpled. Your hair is full of straw. You can't go to school looking like that."

"I can't?" Andi said. Then she grinned. "Good. I'll stay home."

Quick as a wink, Andi jumped out of the buggy.

But Justin was quick too. He grabbed her arm.

"Not so fast, young lady," he said. "Get back in the buggy."

Andi pouted. But she did what her brother told her.

Justin climbed into the buggy and picked up the reins. "Giddy up, Pal," he said.

The horse took off at a fast trot. Away from the ranch.

Andi turned around. She hung on to the

back of the buggy seat and watched the ranch
house get smaller.

She saw Riley carrying firewood for Cook.

She saw her two other big brothers putting
saddles on their horses.

"No fair!" Andi grouched. "Chad and Mitch don't have to go to school."

Just then Melinda pulled Andi around.

"Can't you stay clean for one hour?" she scolded. "You look like a tomboy for the first day of school."

Melinda began to pick the straw out of Andi's hair.

"Stop that!" Andi yanked her braids away.

Justin caught Andi's hand. "There's nothing to be afraid of," he said.

"I'm not afraid!" Andi hollered.

But that wasn't exactly true.

Andi *was* afraid. She did not want to leave the ranch. She did not want to be gone all day in that scary new town called Fresno.

So many strangers! So many buildings! Streets full of horses and wagons.

Worst of all, there would be a school full of strange children. They would all stare at Andi— the youngest pupil.

A shiver went down Andi's neck.

She felt sick inside.

Chapter 2

China Doll or Tomboy?

Justin stopped the buggy in front of a big, white schoolhouse. "Here we are, girls."

Andi stared at her lap.

"Look, Andi." Justin pointed to the roof. "Your school has a new bell."

Andi looked up. Then she shrugged. "It's just a bell."

Justin winked at her. "Miss Hall sometimes lets her pupils ring the bell."

Andi looked at the bell again. It might be fun to ring the bell.

But she didn't tell Justin that. "I want to go home," she said.

"Tell her not to make a fuss, Justin," Melinda begged. She scowled at Andi.

Andi scowled back.

Justin tugged on one of Andi's braids. "Try to act like a little lady today," he said, smiling.

Andi didn't answer.

Melinda hopped down. She put her books in one hand. With her other hand she helped Andi to the ground.

Then she grabbed their lunch pail from the back of the buggy.

Justin waved good-bye and drove away.

"Come on, Andi," Melinda said. "I'm so excited!"

Excited? Andi looked around the schoolyard. *She* was not excited.

Not at all.

A whole bunch of strange boys and girls were laughing and running and shouting. They were all bigger than Andi.

When the children saw Andi, they stopped what they were doing and stared at her.

Andi stared back. *Stop looking at me!*

But she did not say those rude words out loud.

Instead, Andi followed Melinda into the schoolyard.

Even if she didn't want to.

Suddenly, a big girl squealed, "Melinda! I haven't seen you all summer!"

"Sarah!" Melinda squealed back. She set her books and the lunch pail on the ground. Then she raced over to Sarah.

Andi stood frozen. Melinda was leaving!

Wait! Stop! Andi tried to shout.

But the words would not come out. A big lump was stuck in her throat.

All Andi could do was watch those two silly girls.

They hugged. They giggled. They jumped up and down. They whispered.

Then they linked arms and walked back to Andi.

"Your little sister is *adorable*," Sarah told Melinda with a giggle. "And what a darling dress and pinafore! If you brushed out her hair and gave her a big bow, she would look just like a china doll."

Sarah giggled again.

Andi rolled her eyes. Sarah giggled just like Melinda. *Giggle-boxes!*

Andi tugged on Melinda's sleeve. "Tell that girl I like braids best," she whispered.

Melinda shook her head and told Andi to hush.

Andi frowned. Then she dug her hand into her pinafore pocket.

Most of the time, Andi kept special treasures in her overalls pockets. But her overalls were at home. All she had today was a pocket in her new pinafore.

But Andi had put a brand new, extra-special treasure in that pocket just this morning.

She pulled it out.

"My brother Mitch killed a rattlesnake last week," Andi told Sarah. "He cut off the rattle and gave it to me. Mitch says it's the biggest snake he ever saw."

She opened her hand. "See?"

A gray-and-white rattlesnake's rattle lay in Andi's palm. She poked it with her finger. "That brown stuff is dried blood."

Sarah sucked in her breath.

"Do you want to shake it?" Andi asked. She held the rattle up to Sarah.

Sarah backed up. "N-no, thanks!" Then she ran for the schoolhouse.

Melinda put her hands on her hips. "Did you have to show Sarah that *disgusting* snake's rattle?"

"Yep," Andi said, grinning. "Then maybe she won't call me a china doll anymore."

"For sure she won't," Melinda said. "She'll call you a tomboy instead."

Andi put her brand new, extra-special treasure back in her pocket. "Good." She kept smiling.

"You better not show that thing to anybody else," Melinda told her. "Miss Hall will punish you if she sees it."

Just then, the bell began to ring.

A boy stood on the porch. He was pulling a rope. The rope was tied to a big bell on the roof.

Clang, clang!

"Come on," Melinda said. She picked up her books and the lunch pail. Then she took Andi's hand. "School's starting."

Andi hung back. "Do I have to go in there, Melinda?"

Melinda's grumpy voice turned soft. "Yes, you really do. Mother said so. Don't be a scaredy-cat. I'll hold your hand."

"I'm *not* a scaredy-cat!" Andi said.

But that wasn't exactly true.

Chapter 3

Miss Hall

Andi let Melinda drag her up the wooden steps and into the classroom.

The schoolroom was big. Tall windows let the sun in. One wall held a wide blackboard. Just above the blackboard, Andi saw the letters of the alphabet.

I know all those letters, Andi thought.

Melinda tugged on Andi's hand. "Come on. Miss Hall will write down your name and show you where to sit."

"I want to sit with *you*," Andi said.

"You can't," Melinda said. "I sit in the back with the big girls. The little kids sit up front. That's the rule."

"I don't like that rule," Andi said, frowning.

Melinda let out a big breath. "There are a lot of rules you're not going to like."

Just then Miss Hall rapped a ruler on her desk. "Take your seats, please," she said.

Everybody obeyed. Everybody but Melinda and Andi.

Andi stared at Miss Hall. "She's *old*," she whispered to Melinda.

Melinda pinched Andi. That meant, *Be quiet!*

So Andi stopped talking.

But she didn't stop looking at the teacher . . . or thinking about her.

Andi knew some old ladies were nice, like Mrs. Clark.

Mrs. Clark helped Mother with the washing. She always kept lemon drops in her apron pocket for Andi.

But some old ladies were mean, like Aunt Rebecca.

When grumpy Aunt Rebecca came for a visit, she always scolded Andi.

Andi didn't know which kind of old lady Miss Hall was.

Melinda led Andi to the front of the classroom.

"This is my little sister," she told the teacher. "It's her first day of school, and she doesn't know where to sit. Her name is Andrea."

"My name's *Andi*," Andi said quickly. "Just Mother calls me Andrea."

Miss Hall frowned. "You must not talk back, Andrea."

Andi gulped. *Talk back?* She was just telling the teacher her name.

What was so wrong about that?

"You may take your seat," Miss Hall told Melinda.

Andi did not want her big sister to sit down. She squeezed Melinda's hand and held on tight.

It was no use. Melinda peeled Andi's fingers away.

"I have to obey the teacher," she whispered in Andi's ear. "And so do you."

Andi watched Melinda slide into a back seat next to Sarah.

When Andi turned around, Miss Hall was smiling at her. "Since you are the youngest pupil, you will sit right here in the front row."

Andi looked at her new desk. There was room for two children, but the seat was empty.

Andi did not want to sit all by herself.

"I . . . I want to sit with Melinda," she said in a small voice.

Miss Hall's smile turned to a frown. "You must sit where I tell you, Andrea."

Andi didn't want to obey, but she had to. If the teacher said *sit*, then Andi had to sit.

And that was that.

When Andi sat down, Miss Hall stood up. She opened the Bible and read for a long time.

Then the class stood up and sang "America."

Everybody knew the words to that song. Everybody but Andi.

After the America song, Miss Hall said a short prayer. Then she talked about the school rules.

There were a lot of rules.

Andi got tired of listening to all those rules. She watched a big, fat fly instead.

The fly was much more interesting than school rules. It buzzed around the teacher's head. It came to rest on top of Miss Hall's gray bun.

Then the fly flew away and landed on the desk across from Andi's.

Whack!

Andi jumped.

A little boy with straw-colored hair sat at the desk. His hand was resting right where that fly had landed.

He lifted his hand from the desk.

The fly was a squished black spot.

Yuck! Andi thought.

Then, *surprise!*

The boy picked up that dead fly and tossed it at Andi. The fly landed on her desk.

Miss Hall didn't even see it. She was too busy reading all those rules.

"My name's Cory," the boy whispered to Andi. "And I like you."

Andi looked at the squished black spot on her desk. Then she picked up the fly by one wing.

"Throwing dead flies is not a good way to show that you like me," she whispered. "Let's see how *you* like dead flies."

She threw it back at the boy.

The fly landed in Cory's lap. His eyes got big, and his mouth fell open.

Andi grinned.

Chapter 4

Too Many Rules!

It was the longest morning of Andi's life.

Andi showed Miss Hall her ABCs. She read the four words her friend Riley had taught her last week: *rat*, *fat*, *cat*, and *sat*.

"Very good, Andrea," Miss Hall said with a smile. Then she gave Andi new words to learn.

Andi tried to sound them out. But they didn't say anything interesting.

Andi swung her feet back and forth. She scratched her itchy leg. She wrote the new words on her slate. She rubbed them out and wrote them again.

She yawned. *How long is school, anyway?*

Andi turned around in her seat. "Melinda, when can we go home?"

Four rows back, Melinda was reading a book. She sat up straight when Andi spoke. Her cheeks turned red. She put a finger to her lips and frowned.

That meant, *Be quiet!*

Andi didn't want to be quiet. She was tired of sitting still. Her eyes were tired of looking at words. She wanted to run and play with Riley and Taffy. She wanted to ride Coco, her pony.

Andi wanted to go home.

"Andrea, turn around," Miss Hall said. Her voice did not sound friendly.

Andi obeyed.

Miss Hall looked grumpy. Again. She tapped a ruler on her desk.

"Pupils must not talk during class," the teacher said. "That is a rule."

Andi's heart started to beat fast. She broke one of those rules! That meant a *punishment*.

Riley had told Andi all about punishments. He told her that some mean teachers hit their pupils. With a ruler. Especially when they did not obey the rules.

Andi gulped. *Will Miss Hall hit me with that ruler?*

Miss Hall did *not* hit Andi with her ruler. Instead, she told the class it was time for recess.

Everybody jumped up and headed out the door.

"Hooray for recess!" Andi said.

"Andrea, you must stay inside and copy a rule," Miss Hall told her. "Then you will not forget it."

The teacher wrote I WILL NOT TALK DURING CLASS on the blackboard. She read each word out loud to Andi.

"Oh, I don't need to copy that rule," Andi said. "I won't forget it now."

Miss Hall gave Andi a frown. A frown that meant, *Obey!*

So Andi copied the rule. It took a long time. Her fingers got full of white chalk dust.

She sneezed. *Ah-choo!*

"You may go out for recess," Miss Hall said at last.

Andi ran out of that classroom as fast as she could.

"Melinda!" she hollered.

But Melinda was not there.

Then Andi saw three girls. They were playing with a rope.

A girl with brown braids held one end of the rope. Another girl held the other end. They were turning the rope so that it made a big loop in the air.

Just then, a girl with black curls ran under the rope and jumped.

Andi gasped. She had never seen a rope used like this before! A rope was for lassoing a calf or a wild pony—not for jumping.

Andi forgot to be afraid. Jumping over a rope looked like great fun.

She ran over to the girls. "Can I jump?"

"You're too little," the girl with brown braids said.

"I am *not* too little!" Andi said.

Why did everybody always say she was too little?

Before the girls could stop her, Andi ran under the rope and jumped. She jumped fast.

Only, Andi was not fast enough. The rope slapped her legs.

Thud!

Andi tumbled to the ground. Dust flew up.

The girls giggled.

Andi jumped up in surprise. Her legs stung. Her face felt hot.

What had gone wrong?

"I want to try it again," Andi said. "This time I'll do it right."

But the rope tripped Andi again. She hit the ground with another *thud*.

Melinda ran up just then. She pulled Andi to her feet and brushed her off.

"Just look at you!" Melinda scolded. "Your face is dirty, and your new dress is full of dust. You're not acting like a lady. What will Mother say?"

"I don't care!" Andi yelled at Melinda. "School is terrible. Miss Hall is mean. And jumping rope is the worst thing in the world!"

Andi shoved Melinda away. Then she ran to a tall oak tree in the middle of the school-yard.

"Maybe I can't jump that ol' rope, but I can climb a tree," Andi hollered.

"No, Andi!" Melinda shouted. "You can't climb trees at school!"

Andi pretended not to hear Melinda. She pulled herself up on the lowest branch. Then she scrambled to the top of the tree.

Just like that.

"Come down before Miss Hall sees you up there," Melinda called up into the tree. "I'm sorry I yelled at you. Please come down! I'll help you jump rope. I won't let anybody laugh at you."

"I'm staying up here till school's out," Andi said.

"That's what *you* think," Melinda said. "You're going to be in so much trouble."

Andi didn't care.

Not one little bit.

Chapter 5

Tree Trouble

After recess, Andi was still in the tree. Nothing Miss Hall said could talk Andi into coming down.

Andi sat in the tree and didn't say a word.

Finally, the teacher spoke to Melinda. "This has never happened in my school before. Your sister has put herself in real danger."

"Don't worry, Miss Hall," Melinda said. "Andi won't fall out of the tree. She's never even fallen off a galloping horse."

"Perhaps she climbed so high that she's afraid to come down," Miss Hall said in a worried voice.

"No," Melinda told her, "Andi climbs trees all the time. And she's not afraid of anything."

I am too, Andi thought. *I'm afraid of Henry the Eighth. But I'd rather go home and get pecked by that mean old rooster than stay at this school.*

Andi slumped against a branch. "I guess I really *am* a scaredy-cat," she whispered to herself.

"This is an exciting first day of school," a boy named Johnny said. "I hope that girl never comes down."

Andi peeked through the leaves. All of Miss Hall's pupils stood around the tree, watching.

Melinda sighed. "Do you want me to climb up and get her?" She did not sound excited about that idea.

Miss Hall gasped. "Goodness, no! I don't want two pupils stuck in a tree."

Andi was glad Miss Hall said that. Melinda was a very good tree climber. Andi did not want her sister climbing up after her.

"Should I get my brother?" Melinda asked. "He'll make her come down. Ever since Father died, Justin has sort of taken over. Andi minds him . . . most of the time."

Miss Hall nodded. "If that is the only way."

Then she clapped her hands. "The rest of you pupils! Back to class."

Nobody wanted to go back to class. They moaned and groaned, but they all obeyed.

Except Cory the fly killer. He hid behind the tree.

"Hey, Andi!" Cory called when everybody left. "You're the only girl I know who's not scared of dead flies. And you can climb a tree besides. Do you want to be friends?"

Andi looked at the boy with hair like yellow straw. He was grinning. A front tooth was missing.

"Maybe," Andi said.

Cory waved and ran back to class.

⇢ ⇠

Andi liked sitting in the tree. It was cool and shady. Every few minutes, a breeze stirred the leaves.

She pulled the snake's rattle from her pocket and shook it. The rattle made a dry, rustling noise.

She smiled.

"Andi."

Andi pushed the leaves away and looked down.

Justin was standing next to the tree. He looked grumpy.

Very grumpy.

Andi stopped smiling.

"Andi," Justin said, "I want you to come down."

"I'm staying up here till school's out," Andi said. "I don't like school. Not one little bit. Miss Hall gave me a punishment. And I didn't even know I broke that ol' rule."

Justin let out a big breath. "Young lady, I have to be in the courtroom in fifteen minutes. The judge will not be happy if I'm late. For the last time, *come down*."

Andi bit her lip. Justin sounded worse than grumpy. He sounded like he might climb up after her.

That would not be good.

Andi put her special treasure back in her pocket. She climbed down a few branches.

"Don't you want to know why I'm up here?" she asked.

"You can tell me about it later," Justin said.

"Right now, it doesn't matter. Your teacher told you to come down, and you didn't obey her."

Andi climbed down a few more branches.

Suddenly, a branch snagged Andi's new pinafore. It tore her pocket open with a loud *rip*.

"My rattle!" Andi let go of the branch and tried to catch her treasure.

Too late. The rattle dropped to the ground at Justin's feet.

Then *crash!*

Andi tumbled down, down, down.

A branch slapped her in the face. Another branch hit her on the arm.

Plop!

She fell into Justin's arms.

Justin hugged her tight. "That was close. You could have landed on your head."

Andi's cheek stung, but she didn't say a word. She was looking at the rip in her pinafore.

Uh-oh!

Justin set her on the ground and brushed her off.

"I never want to see you in this tree again," he said. "Now get back to school."

Andi scooped up her special rattle and ran.

Chapter 6

Tardy Means Late

Andi felt grumpy the rest of the day.

"Everybody's mad at me," she grouched.

Mother scolded Andi for not obeying the teacher. She scolded her for ripping her clothes.

"And now I have to mend your pinafore," Mother said with a sigh.

After supper, Melinda told Andi she was the worst tomboy in all of California.

Even Justin shook his head when Andi told him why she had climbed that tree.

But the first day of school was over. Andi was glad about that.

At breakfast the next morning, Andi asked, "How many more days of school are there?"

Chad laughed. "A lot more than *you* can count, little sister."

Andi slumped in her chair. She could count all the way to one hundred.

Just then Melinda walked into the dining room. She was still dressed in her nightgown. Her cheeks were bright red.

"I don't feel good," Melinda moaned. "My throat hurts."

Mother felt Melinda's forehead. "You have a fever, sweetheart. Go back to bed. I'll come up later."

Andi dropped her spoon at this news. "Melinda's not going to school?"

"She's sick," Mother explained.

No school! No school! Hooray for a sick sister! Andi's thoughts buzzed around inside her head like busy bees.

Now Andi could play with Riley. Riley would ride Midnight, his big, black horse. Andi would ride Coco. And Taffy would come along.

Andi wiggled with happy thoughts. *And maybe Riley knows how to jump that rope. He can show me—*

"Are you ready for school, Andi?" Justin

asked. He pushed back his chair and stood up. "It's time to go."

Andi's happy thoughts went *crash!*

"But . . . I thought . . ." Andi stopped talking. A big lump was sneaking into her throat.

"*What* did you think?" Mother asked.

Andi swallowed the lump. "Melinda's sick. She's not going to school. So I'm not going to school either."

Mother looked puzzled. "You're not sick, Andrea. Why should you stay home?"

Now Andi felt *very* sick. But not the kind of sick that would keep her home from school.

"I can't go to school by myself," she said.

"Yes, you can," Mother told her. "You're a big girl now. Go with Justin. You don't want to be late."

I don't care if I'm late, Andi thought. But she didn't say it out loud. That was called *talking back*.

And talking back always got Andi into trouble.

"Yes, Mother," she said instead.

Andi felt all shivery inside. Today, Melinda would not be there to hold her hand.

Andi would have to go to school . . . alone.

When Andi got to school, a tall girl was ringing the school bell.

"I think that's the second bell," Justin said. "You better run, or you'll be marked tardy."

Andi didn't want to run. She didn't even want to get out of the buggy.

"What's 'tardy'?" she asked.

Justin lifted her out of the buggy. "It means late. Now get going."

Andi did *not* get going. She stood and watched Justin drive away. Then she kicked at the dust. It puffed up, all over her new shoes.

Andi liked the way the dust puffed up.

She stomped to the schoolhouse. Each step made a dusty puff.

But Andi did not stomp into the classroom. She walked to her seat as quiet as a mouse.

Miss Hall was reading from the Bible. She looked up.

"I must mark you tardy, Andrea," she said. "If you're late again, you will be punished."

Miss Hall closed the Bible and put it away. Then she walked over to the blackboard and

began writing down a whole bunch of number problems.

Andi's stomach felt like a tight knot. No wonder Justin had told her to run! She had broken another rule.

How many of those things are there? she wondered.

No turning around. No climbing trees. No being late. No talking. No . . .

Psst.

Andi jumped at the sound.

"Look what I have," the boy named Cory whispered.

Andi leaned close to see.

Cory opened his hands. Inside was a brown lizard. It had a blue belly.

"Oh!" Andi gasped.

"You're not scared?" Cory asked.

Andi forgot about the no-talking rule. "No. I like lizards."

Cory grinned. "His name is Pickles."

Just then Miss Hall said, "Cory, bring me what you have in your hands."

Andi looked up. Miss Hall was back at her desk already.

Uh-oh!

Cory let out a big sigh. "Yes, ma'am." He gave Andi a sad look and walked up to the teacher's desk.

"I've told you many times to leave your playthings at home," Miss Hall scolded.

She reached across her desk and gently began to pry open Cory's fingers.

Free at last, the lizard with the blue belly raced across the desk.

Right into the teacher's lap.

Chapter 7

Runaway Lizard

Miss Hall shrieked. She leaped from her chair.

The lizard fell to the floor and raced across the wooden boards.

"Catch him!" Cory shouted. "Don't let him get away!"

"Where is he?" a boy yelled.

The lizard zipped under the teacher's desk.

The boys ran around the room shouting. The girls ran around the room screaming.

Miss Hall rapped her desk with a ruler. "Sit down!" she yelled.

No one paid any attention.

Then Andi saw the lizard. He ran out from under Miss Hall's desk. He came closer and closer, until he was right by Andi's feet.

Andi sat as still as a fence post.

The boys looked under desks.

They peeked around the woodstove at the back of the schoolroom.

They pulled the broom out of a corner and looked there.

Andi giggled. The boys were looking in all the wrong places!

She reached under her desk and scooped up the lizard.

Just like that.

Andi looked around for Miss Hall.

The teacher was still rapping her desk with that ruler. But it looked like most of the children were going back to their seats.

Nobody was screaming anymore.

"Here's your lizard," Andi told Cory.

Cory looked up from the floor. "Thanks, Andi."

Andi dropped the lizard into Cory's hands. "Why did you bring a lizard to school? It's probably breaking a rule."

"Bringing pets to school is breaking a *big* rule," Cory said. "But I brought Pickles for you. On account of you looked so lonely sitting by yourself. Pickles could hide in your desk and keep you company."

"Really?" Andi looked at the lizard named Pickles. Then she smiled at Cory.

Cory smiled back.

Miss Hall finally sat down at her desk. She was breathing hard. She wiped her forehead with a handkerchief.

"Cory, get rid of that thing," she said in a shaky voice.

Cory's smiley face turned sad. "Yes, ma'am," he said and left the classroom.

A few minutes later, Cory came back. His hands were shoved in his pockets. He slumped in his seat and stared at the desktop. He sighed.

Andi felt sorry for Cory. He had been kind to her. He had made her forget about being scared of school. His lizard had made her laugh.

"I'll be your friend," Andi whispered to Cory. "I'll help you catch another lizard."

Before Cory could answer, Miss Hall scolded him some more.

"Shame on you, young man," she said. "Now go stand in the corner."

Andi felt scary shivers go down her neck. The corner was at the front of the classroom.

Right where everybody could look at you and laugh.

Poor Cory.

Cory stood up. He didn't look scared at all. "Yes, ma'am."

Cory took his hands out of his pockets. Then he walked past Andi's desk and opened his hand.

Plop!

Cory's lizard fell into Andi's lap.

Cory grinned. Then he hurried to the corner.

Andi clapped one hand over her mouth. She dropped her other hand over the wiggling lizard.

She tried not to giggle.

"Stay still," she whispered between her fingers.

But the lizard did not stay still. He didn't like being squished in Andi's lap.

He wanted out.

Andi's heart began to thump fast. She put both hands over the lizard.

Only, that didn't work either. Pickles was too wiggly.

He slipped between Andi's fingers and

climbed up, up, up. Right up the front of her pinafore.

Andi gasped. She tried not to, but that gasp just sneaked out.

Miss Hall looked at Andi. Then she stood up fast. "Oh, my!"

Just then the lizard jumped onto one of Andi's braids. Up, up, up he went. Clear to the top of Andi's head.

"My goodness!" Miss Hall said. Her eyes opened wide.

The children began to laugh.

Cory peeked out from his corner and laughed too.

Andi's heart was pounding. *This is not even funny!*

She wanted to crawl under her desk and hide from those laughing kids.

The teacher rapped her ruler on her desk. Her voice turned growly. "That's enough, children. Settle down."

Miss Hall frowned at Andi. "I'm afraid you must stand in a corner too, Andrea. But first you will throw that lizard out. And I mean *right now*."

Andi jumped up quick as a jack-in-the-box.

She snatched Pickles off her head and ran outside. Her feet clattered down the wooden steps.

The corner!

"This is not even my own fault," Andi told herself. "Miss Hall is a mean old lady. And . . . and . . . I'm not going back to that school."

Andi ran.

And she didn't look back.

Chapter 8

Runaway Pupil

Thump, thump, thump! Andi's feet clomped down the wooden sidewalk. "Not going back, not going back," she chanted as she ran.

Soon Andi couldn't see the schoolhouse. She couldn't see the schoolyard.

Andi took a deep breath and tried to run another block. But the blocks in this town were too long. They seemed to go on forever.

Andi stopped running. The sun was burning her head. She felt thirsty.

"I'm hot," she told Pickles.

Pickles lay still. *Very* still. Andi was squeezing the lizard a little too tight. She didn't want him to get away this time.

"I'll take you to Justin," Andi said. "I'll tell

him how terrible school is. He'll take us back to the ranch. You'll be safe there. And I won't have to stand in the corner."

She wrinkled her eyebrows, thinking. "I just have to find out where Justin works. That's all. It's in a place called a *law office*."

Pickles didn't move.

Andi looked up and down the busy street. It was filled with buggies and farm wagons. Cowboys on fast horses galloped by. Dust flew up.

Andi sneezed.

All the buildings looked alike. Most of them had big signs with words on them.

Andi tried to read the words. "B-A-N-K," she spelled. "H-O-T-E-L." But she didn't know what the words said.

"I wish that boy Cory was here," Andi said. "Cory can read. He could help me find Justin."

She sat down on the wooden sidewalk to rest and think some more.

Then Andi looked at Pickles. "Poor lizard. You look squished. But if I let you go, a wagon or a horse might run over you."

She shook her head. "Then you'd *really* be squished."

Just then Andi thought of an idea. An *excellent* idea. Something that would keep Pickles from getting squished.

Andi yanked her hair ribbon out. Carefully, she wrapped one end of the ribbon around the lizard's belly. She tied it in a knot.

"Now you are almost exactly like a dog," Andi said. "But you're a lizard. A lizard on a leash."

For a few minutes, Andi let Pickles run around on the wooden sidewalk. But then he almost fell into a big crack between the boards.

So Andi picked him up. "We have to find Justin," she said.

Andi walked down another long block. But she still couldn't find Justin's law office.

"We're lost," she told Pickles. "This town is too big."

Andi's stomach felt fluttery. Those butterflies were back.

Being lost was a scary feeling.

Just then, Andi heard horses. They were snorting and whinnying.

She looked around. Right next to her stood a building. It was just like a big barn. The double doors hung open.

The horse sounds were coming from inside that barn.

Andi's heart thumped hard. But this time it was not a scary thumping.

Andi was not afraid of horses. Not one bit. Horses were not the same thing as strangers. Andi loved horses.

So she went inside the barn.

"Oh, my!" Andi whispered.

Everywhere she looked, Andi saw horses in stalls. She had never seen so many horses inside a barn at one time. Most of the horses on the Circle C ranch lived outdoors.

"What pretty horses!" Andi said.

She saw brown horses, black horses, and spotted horses. She even saw a golden horse like Taffy.

Andi forgot about being lost. She forgot about being afraid.

She even forgot about her bad morning at school.

Andi held Pickles and walked over to one of the stalls.

"What's your name?" she asked a brown horse with a black mane. She reached out her hand.

The horse poked his head over the half-door. He nibbled Andi's palm.

Andi stuffed Pickles in her pinafore pocket. Then she opened the stall door and stepped inside. She patted the horse.

The horse backed up at her touch. He laid his ears back and snorted.

"Easy, big fella," Andi told the horse. That's what Chad said whenever a horse acted up. "I'm not going to hurt you."

The horse flicked his ears forward at the sound of Andi's voice. He settled right down.

"That's better," Andi said. She ran her hand along his neck.

The horse blew out a soft horsey breath at Andi.

She rubbed his nose and laughed. "I think I'll stay here all day."

Then all of a sudden an angry voice shouted, "Who's there?"

Chapter 9

Horse Thief

Andi's heart did a great big skip at that scary voice.

She backed up against the wall and slid down in the straw.

"I know you're in here," the man said. "I won't stand for horse thieves in my livery stable. Come out real peaceful-like, and we'll go see the sheriff."

Andi felt shaky inside. *I'm not a horse thief!*

She crawled into a corner and held Pickles extra tight.

Maybe that man won't see me back here, she thought.

Andi squeezed her eyes shut. "Please, God," she whispered, "Don't let that man take me to the sheriff. I'm sorry I ran away. I wish I was back in school."

Then Andi heard a soft chuckle.

"Well, well, what do we have here?" The voice didn't sound angry now. Or scary.

Andi opened her eyes and looked up.

A large man stood right above her. One hand was resting on the horse's back. His other hand held a big, wooden stick.

"You're the littlest horse thief I ever saw," he said with a laugh.

The man dropped the stick and lifted Andi to her feet. Then he led her outside.

"What are you doing in here?" he asked. "This is no place for a little girl. You could get kicked or bit or stomped on."

Andi didn't answer. Her tongue was stuck.

The man kneeled down beside her. "I didn't mean to scare you. Tell me who you are and I'll find your folks. Are you lost?"

Andi wanted to tell him yes, she *was* lost. But she couldn't make her tongue say those words.

Then *clomp, clomp, clomp.* Someone came running up the wooden sidewalk.

It was Cory. He was panting hard.

"I've been looking all over town for you, Andi," Cory said. "Miss Hall told me to find you. She's really worried—crying almost."

"You know this girl?" the big man asked.

"Sure I do, Pa," Cory said. "She's my new friend, Andi Carter. She doesn't like school very much. She ran off 'cause Miss Hall sent her to the corner."

Cory ducked his head. "Only, that was my fault. On account of me taking Pickles to school."

Cory's father sighed when he heard that.

Then he stood up and said, "Your little friend was in Thunder's stall. She could have been badly hurt."

Cory turned to Andi. "This is my pa, Mr. Blake. You don't need to be scared of him. And none of our horses would hurt a fly."

Mr. Blake ruffled Cory's hair. "You two wait inside while I find Andi's brother. We need to get you back to class. Poor Miss Hall. It's only the second day of school."

He chuckled and walked away.

Cory took Andi inside to his family's cozy kitchen. It smelled just like warm cookies.

Cory's mother gave them cookies to eat. And milk to drink.

The cookies and milk helped Andi's tongue get unstuck.

"I don't want to go back to school," she told Cory. "Miss Hall is mean and scary. I don't want to stand in the corner."

Cory shook his head.

"You got it all wrong, Andi," he said. "Miss Hall is *nice*. She never hits anybody with her ruler. She only hits her desk. She scolds a lot, but you get used to that. Sending you to the corner is the worst thing she'll ever do."

Cory's voice changed to a whisper. "Don't tell Miss Hall, but I *like* the corner. It's right next to the window. I can see a lot out there."

Andi's eyes opened wide at this news. "You *like* standing in the corner?"

Cory nodded. "Sometimes I get tired of doing lessons. Then I act up, so I can go look out the window."

Andi wrinkled her eyebrows and thought about what Cory said.

I'm afraid of being sent to the corner. Cory likes it.

"You're kind of crazy," she finally told him.

Andi suddenly didn't feel very scared about school anymore.

She untied the ribbon from around the lizard's belly. "You can have Pickles back now."

Cory found a small box with a lid. He dropped Pickles in. "No, I gave him to you."

He handed Andi the box. "He's real easy to keep. He eats bugs and ants. And he specially likes spiders."

Andi gave Cory an extra-big smile. "I'll take good care of Pickles. And he can be both of ours. I'll keep him sometimes, and you can keep him sometimes."

Then Andi thought of one more thing to tell Cory. "Thanks for making me feel better about school. I think I'm ready to go back now."

"Well, that's certainly good news," Justin said.

Andi spun around. Her brother and Mr. Blake were standing in the doorway.

Chapter 10

Back to School

Justin had his arms crossed. He was frowning.

That meant, *You are in big trouble, young lady.*

"I'm not in the tree, Justin," Andi said in a tiny voice. "You said you never wanted to see me in that tree again. Remember? And I didn't climb it. I stayed right on the ground this time."

Justin dropped his arms to his sides.

"That's true," he said. "But you ran away from school. And you walked around town by yourself."

He let out a big breath. "What on earth got into you?"

Andi shrugged. She did not want to be scolded in front of Cory's whole entire family.

Justin took her hand. "Come on. We can talk about it on the way back to school."

Andi picked up the box with Pickles, told Mrs. Blake thank-you for the cookies, and went with her brother.

Then Andi talked.

She told Justin about being tardy and about Cory's lizard.

And about the lizard climbing on her head.

And about the kids laughing.

And about Miss Hall getting upset and sending her to the corner.

Justin listened.

"Only that wasn't even my fault, Justin," Andi said. "So I *had* to run. I had to find you. I was scared."

Andi finished talking and looked at the ground. She didn't want to see Justin's face. He was probably still mad.

Then Andi got a surprise.

Justin stopped walking. He picked Andi up and hugged her. "Are you still scared, honey?"

Andi shook her head. "No. Well . . . maybe a little. But Cory helped me feel better."

"I told you yesterday there was nothing to be afraid of," Justin said.

"I know. And I already told God I'm sorry for running away. So now I'll tell you."

Andi sighed. "Sorry, Justin. Sorry for running away."

Justin patted Andi on the back and set her down.

"I forgive you," he told her. "But now you have to tell Miss Hall you're sorry."

He pointed at the schoolyard. "Look. It's recess. You and Miss Hall can have a little chat all by yourselves."

"By myself?" Andi asked. "Can't you come with me?"

Justin kneeled down beside Andi.

"I think you should let God go with you," he said. "He'll help you do this. Then I don't think you'll ever be afraid of Miss Hall again. Or of school either."

Andi looked at the schoolhouse. She looked at her feet. Then she looked at her brother.

"Okay, Justin," she said at last. "I'll do it. But can you do something for me?"

Justin nodded. "Sure."

Andi handed him the lizard box. "Take care of Pickles. You can keep him on your desk in your law-office place until after school."

"Is this what I think it is?" Justin asked.

Andi grinned. "Cory's lizard. Only he's mine now."

She dashed across the yard and into the schoolhouse.

Miss Hall was sitting at her desk. When she saw Andi, she smiled.

That made it easier for Andi to say she was sorry.

Then the teacher said, "Cory told me that the lizard on your head was not your fault. I'm sorry I blamed you."

Miss Hall was sorry too? That made Andi feel warm inside.

Maybe Miss Hall *was* a nice old lady like Cory said.

"I know yesterday and today have been hard for you, Andrea," Miss Hall was saying. "There are a lot of rules to remember. But you will learn to like school. I promise."

Andi wasn't so sure about that.

Miss Hall stood up. "How would you like

to ring the bell to call the children in from recess?"

Andi's heart did a little skip. A happy skip this time. "Me?"

"Yes, indeed," Miss Hall said. Her eyes looked twinkly.

"Oh, yes, ma'am!" Andi said.

Andi didn't wait for Miss Hall. She ran to the porch and took hold of the rope.

Clang, clang, clang!

Maybe school wasn't so bad, after all.

A Peek into the Past

What was school *really* like in 1874?

The teacher began each day by reading from the Bible. Sometimes the children sang a patriotic song, like "America" ("My Country, 'Tis of Thee"). Nobody said the Pledge of Allegiance. *Why didn't they say the Pledge to the flag?* They couldn't say it because the pledge was not written until 1892.

Children of all ages studied in the same room. Some pupils were only five years old. Some were eighteen years old. *What was good about that?* Older students could help the younger children. *What was bad about that?*

Some older boys were bigger than the teacher and did not obey. They were bullies.

Most schoolteachers were very strict in 1874. There were a lot of rules. If students broke a rule, they might be spanked. Here are a few rules and the number of swats for breaking them:

Calling each other bad names	3 swats
Telling lies	7 swats
Fighting	5 swats
Wearing long fingernails	2 swats
Splashing each other at playtime	2 swats
Having dirty hands and face	2 swats

Do some of these rules sound mean? There were even rules about not climbing trees.

It was hard to sit still all day long. And it was no fun to be scolded or sent to the corner in front of the entire class. But most children in 1874 liked going to school. They enjoyed being with their friends. They knew learning was important.

Susan K. Marlow, like Andi, has an imagination that never stops! She enjoys teaching writing workshops, sharing what she's learned as a homeschooling mom, and relaxing on her 14-acre homestead in the great state of Washington.

Leslie Gammelgaard, blessed by the tall trees and flower gardens that surround her home in Washington state, finds inspiration for her artwork in the antics of her lively little granddaughter.

Grow Up with Andi!

Don't miss any of Andi's adventures in the Circle C Beginnings series

Andi's Pony Trouble
Andi's Indian Summer
Andi's Fair Surprise
Andi's Scary School Days
Andi's Lonely Little Foal
Andi's Circle C Christmas

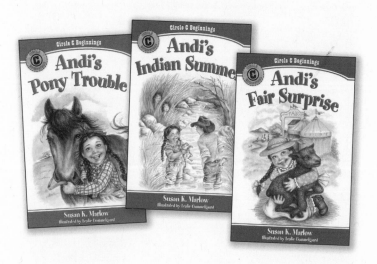

And you can visit www.AndiandTaffy.com
for free coloring pages, learning activities,
puzzles you can do online, and more!

For readers ages 9-14!

Andi's adventures continue in the Circle C Adventures series

Andrea Carter and the Long Ride Home
Andrea Carter and the Dangerous Decision
Andrea Carter and the Family Secret
Andrea Carter and the San Francisco Smugglers
Andrea Carter and the Trouble with Treasure
Andrea Carter and the Price of Truth

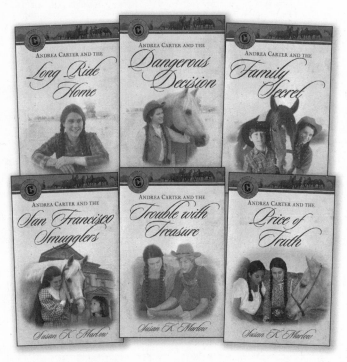

**Check out Andi's Web site at
www.CircleCAdventures.com**